POOH'S POEMS

POOH'S POEMS

A. A. MILNE

illustrated by
ERNEST H. SHEPARD

TED SMART

POOH'S POEMS

Winnie-the-Pooh may be a Bear of Very Little Brain, but he is always making up poems and songs and little rhymes.

Poems are Pooh's way of trying to think what to do about honey or the weather or situations.

"It isn't Brain, because You Know Why, but it comes to me sometimes," says Pooh.

For Pooh the best way to write Poetry and Hums is letting things come to him. Poetry and Hums aren't things which you get, they're things which get *you*. All you can do is go where they can find you.

And so Pooh may be just walking through the Forest humming proudly to himself when he will suddenly think of a new verse to make into a Hum to sing or a Poem to solve a problem.

"Pooh is inspired by a hum or a whistle he hears in the tops of the trees. "

A.A.MILNE

SING HO! FOR THE LIFE OF A BEAR

Sing Ho! for the life of a Bear!
Sing Ho! for the life of a Bear!
I don't much mind if it rains or snows,
'Cos I've got a lot of honey on my nice new nose!
I don't much care if it snows or thaws,
'Cos I've got a lot of honey on my nice clean paws!
Sing Ho! for a Bear!
Sing Ho! for a Pooh!
And I'll have a little something in an hour or two!

ISN'T IT FUNNY

Isn't it funny
How a bear likes honey?
Buzz! Buzz! Buzz!
I wonder why he does?

HOW SWEET TO BE
A CLOUD

How sweet to be a cloud
    Floating in the Blue!
Every little cloud
Always sings aloud.

'How sweet to be a cloud
    Floating in the Blue!'
It makes him very proud
To be a little cloud.

IF BEARS WERE BEES

It's a very funny thought that, if Bears were Bees,
They'd build their nests at the *bottom* of trees.
And that being so (if the Bees were Bears),
We shouldn't have to climb up all these stairs.

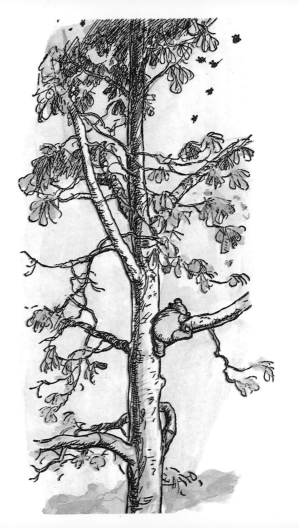

HUNNY

It's very, very funny,
'Cos I *know* I had some honey;
'Cos it had a label on,
   Saying HUNNY.

A goloptious full-up pot too,
And I don't know where it's got to,
No, I don't know where it's gone –
   Well, it's funny.

FOR STOUTNESS
EXERCISES

Tra-la-la, tra-la-la,
Tra-la-la, tra-la-la,
Rum-tum-tiddle-um-tum.
Tiddle-iddle, tiddle-iddle,
Tiddle-iddle, tiddle-iddle,
Rum-tum-tum-tiddle-um.

ANXIOUS POOH SONG

3 Cheers for Pooh!
(*For Who?*)
For Pooh –
(*Why what did he do?*)
I thought you knew;
He saved his friend from a wetting!
3 Cheers for Bear!
(*For where?*)
For Bear –
He couldn't swim,
But he rescued him!
(*He rescued who?*)
Oh, listen, do!
I am talking of Pooh –
(*Of who?*)
Of Pooh!
(*I'm sorry I keep forgetting*).
Well, Pooh was a Bear of Enormous Brain –
(*Just say it again!*)
Of enormous brain –
(*Of enormous what!*)
Well, he ate a lot,
And I don't know if he could swim or not,
But he managed to float

On a sort of boat
(*On a sort of what!*)
Well, a sort of pot –
So now let's give him three hearty cheers
(*So now let's give him three hearty whiches!*)
And hope he'll be with us for years and years,
And grow in health and wisdom and riches!
3 Cheers for Pooh!
(*For who?*)
For Pooh –
3 Cheers for Bear!
(*For where?*)
For Bear –
3 Cheers for the wonderful Winnie-the-Pooh!
(*Just tell me, somebody* – WHAT DID HE DO?)

HERE LIES A TREE

Here lies a tree which Owl (a bird)
  Was fond of when it stood on end,
  And Owl was talking to a friend
Called Me (in case you hadn't heard)
When something Oo occurred.

For lo! the wind was blusterous
  And flattened out his favourite tree;
  And things looked bad for him and we –
Looked bad, I mean, for he and us –
I've never known them wuss.

The Piglet (PIGLET) thought a thing:
  'Courage!' he said. 'There's always hope.
  I want a thinnish piece of rope.
Or, if there isn't any, bring
A thickish piece of string.'

So to the letter-box he rose,
  While Pooh and Owl said 'Oh!' and 'Hum!'
  And where the letters always come
(Called 'LETTERS ONLY') Piglet sqoze
His head and then his toes.

O gallant Piglet (PIGLET)! Ho!
　　Did Piglet tremble? Did he blinch?
　　No, no, he struggled inch by inch
Through LETTERS ONLY, as I know
Because I saw him go.

He ran and ran, and then he stood
　　And shouted, 'Help for Owl, a bird,
　　And Pooh, a bear!' until he heard
The others coming through the wood
As quickly as they could.

'Help-help and Rescue!' Piglet cried,
　　And showed the others where to go.
　　[Sing ho! for Piglet (PIGLET) ho!]
And soon the door was opened wide,
And we were both outside!

Sing ho! for Piglet, ho!
Ho!

I LAY ON MY CHEST

I lay on my chest
And I thought it best
To pretend I was having an evening rest;
I lay on my tum
And I tried to hum
But nothing particular seemed to come.
My face was flat
On the floor, and that
Is all very well for an acrobat;
But it doesn't seem fair
To a Friendly Bear
To stiffen him out with a basket-chair.
And a sort of sqoze
Which grows and grows
Is not too nice for his poor old nose,
And a sort of squch
Is much too much
For his neck and his mouth
    and his ears and such.

POOR LITTLE TIGGER

What shall we do about poor little Tigger?
If he never eats nothing he'll never get bigger.
He doesn't like honey and haycorns and thistles
Because of the taste and because of the bristles.
And all the good things which an animal likes
Have the wrong sort of swallow or too many spikes.
But whatever his weight in pounds, shillings, and
    ounces,
He always seems bigger because of his bounces.

RABBIT

If Rabbit
Was bigger
And fatter
And stronger,
Or bigger
Than Tigger,
If Tigger was smaller,
Then Tigger's bad habit
Of bouncing at Rabbit
Would matter
No longer,
If Rabbit
Was taller.

THE MORE IT SNOWS

The more it
SNOWS-tiddely-pom,
The more it
GOES-tiddely-pom
The more it
GOES-tiddely-pom
On
Snowing.

And nobody
KNOWS-tiddely-pom
How cold my
TOES-tiddely-pom
How cold my
TOES-tiddely-pom
Are
Growing.

LINES WRITTEN BY
A BEAR OF VERY LITTLE BRAIN

On Monday, when the sun is hot
I wonder to myself a lot:
'Now is it true, or is it not,
'That what is which and which is what?'

On Tuesday, when it hails and snows,
The feeling on me grows and grows
That hardly anybody knows
If those are these or these are those.

On Wednesday, when the sky is blue,
And I have nothing else to do,
I sometimes wonder if it's true
That who is what and what is who.

On Thursday, when it starts to freeze
And hoar-frost twinkles on the trees,
How very readily one sees
That these are whose – but whose are these?

On Friday –

THIS WARM AND SUNNY SPOT

This warm and sunny Spot
    Belongs to Pooh.
And here he wonders what
    He's going to do.
Oh, bother, I forgot –
    It's Piglet's too.

EXPOTITION TO THE
NORTH POLE

They all went off to discover the Pole,
    Owl and Piglet and Rabbit and all;
It's a Thing you Discover, as I've been tole
    By Owl and Piglet and Rabbit and all.
Eeyore, Christopher Robin and Pooh
And Rabbit's relations all went too –
And where the Pole was none of them knew . . .
    Sing Hey! for Owl and Rabbit and all.

COTTLESTON PIE

Cottleston, Cottleston, Cottleston Pie.
A fly can't bird, but a bird can fly.
Ask me a riddle and I reply:
'*Cottleston, Cottleston, Cottleston Pie.*'

Cottleston, Cottleston, Cottleston Pie,
A fish can't whistle and neither can I.
Ask me a riddle and I reply:
'*Cottleston, Cottleston, Cottleston Pie.*'

Cottleston, Cottleston, Cottleston Pie,
Why does a chicken, I don't know why.
Ask me a riddle and I reply:
'*Cottleston, Cottleston, Cottleston Pie.*'

A MYST'RY

Here is a myst'ry
About a little fir-tree.
Owl says it's *his* tree,
And Kanga says it's *her* tree.

NOISE, BY POOH

Oh, the butterflies are flying,
Now the winter days are dying,
And the primroses are trying
   To be seen.
And the turtle-doves are cooing,
And the woods are up and doing,
For the violets are blue-ing
   In the green.

Oh, the honey-bees are gumming
On their little wings, and humming
That the summer, which is coming,
   Will be fun.
And the cows are almost cooing,
And the turtle-doves are mooing,
Which is why a Pooh is poohing
   In the sun.

For the spring is really springing;
You can see a skylark singing,
And the blue-bells, which are ringing,
   Can be heard.
And the cuckoo isn't cooing,
But he's cucking and he's ooing,
And a Pooh is simply poohing
   Like a bird.

I COULD SPEND
A HAPPY MORNING

I could spend a happy morning
    Seeing Roo,
I could spend a happy morning
    Being Pooh.
For it doesn't seem to matter,
If I don't get any fatter
(And I *don't* get any fatter),
    What I do.

Oh, I like his way of talking,
    Yes, I do.
It's the nicest way of talking
    Just for two.
And a Help-yourself with Rabbit
Though it may become a habit,
Is a *pleasant* sort of habit
    For a Pooh.

I could spend a happy morning
    Seeing Piglet.
And I couldn't spend a happy morning
    Not seeing Piglet.
And it doesn't seem to matter
If I don't see Owl and Eeyore (or any of the others),
And I'm not going to see Owl or Eeyore
                              (or any of the others)
            Or Christopher Robin.

THE TAIL

Who found the Tail?
    'I,' said Pooh,
'At a quarter to two
    (Only it was quarter to eleven really),
I found the Tail!'

Pooh's Poems
are taken from *Winnie-the-Pooh*
originally published in Great Britain 14th October 1926
and *The House at Pooh Corner*
originally published in Great Britain 11th October 1928
by Methuen & Co. Ltd.
Text by A.A.Milne and line drawings by Ernest H.Shepard
copyright under the Berne Convention

First published 1991 by Methuen Children's Books
an imprint of Egmont Children's Books Limited
239 Kensington High Street, London W8 6SA

This edition first produced in 1998 for The Book People
Hall Wood Avenue, Haydock, St Helens WA11 9UL

ISBN 1 85613 499 7

3 5 7 9 10 8 6 4

Printed in Hong Kong